FRESHWATER MERMAIDS

Troy Graham

Copyright © 2021 Troy Graham

Special Thanks to Shawn Wolfman for cover art and
Jaymie Depew for peer editing.

All rights reserved

The characters and events portrayed in this book are fictitious. Any similarity to real persons, living or dead, is coincidental and not intended by the author.

No part of this book may be reproduced, or stored in a retrieval system, or transmitted in any form or by any means, electronic, mechanical, photocopying, recording, or otherwise, without express written permission of the publisher.

ISBN-13: 9798719677743

Cover Art by: Shawn Wolfman
Printed in the United States of America

CONTENTS

Title Page	
Copyright	
Fresh Water Mermaids	2
Sunrise	6
Staring	7
Sober October	8
Sister	9
Silhouettes of Dreams	10
Sailboat	11
Romantic	12
Reliable	13
Quotes	14
Public Toilet	15
Porcelain Eyes	16
Pool Cleaner	17
Pandemic	18
Outhouse	19
Orphans of Love	20
Night Thoughts	21
My Cat	22
Moon Glow	23

Mind Games	24
Marble Mask	25
Bleach	26
Christmas in July	27
Cat	28
Change	29
Chalk Drawing	30
Hate	31
Green Candle	32
God's Canvas	33
Go Away	34
Silence	35
Your Body	36
2nd Hand Slumber	37
6 - Word Poems	38
6 - Word Poems (CONT.)	39
Bedroom of Broken Dreams	40
All	41
Bells	42
Bobby Fischer	43
Blue Jay	44
Distance	45
Death	46
Daydreams and Dental Floss	47
Dark Morning	48
Crossing the River	49
Cold Pros	50
Coffin Dust	51

Glass House	52
Forgotten Dreams	53
Flood	54
Finding	55
Face Down	56
Hate pt. 2	57
Life in Mind	58
Lost and Lost	59
Life	60
Lake Superior	61
Ladder	62
Immortal Reality	63
I've Lost My Mind Again	64
I'm Lost	65
The Steeple	66
Your Love	67
Your Eyes	68
Why?	69
Where is the Love?	70
Truths	71
Today	72
Windmill	73
Time	74
The Trembling Wind	75
The Trees	76
Two Roses	77
What the Hell	78
Time Frequency	79

Tower	80
I love you	81
Hopscotch	82
Hope	83
Lost lost lost	84
Lost	85
Take the Time	86
Steam Ghost	87
The Rain	88
The Fifth Floor	89
The Dice You Roll	90
The Tire Swing	91
About The Author	92

FRESH WATER MERMAIDS

I guess I should start off by introducing myself:

My name is Troy Graham and I live in a small town in the Upper Peninsula of Michigan called Marquette and I want to make one thing crystal clear - I'm not crazy or naive, but I do believe in things that I see with my own eyes.

So, I'm here today to tell you with 100% certainty that fresh water mermaids are real.

Now, please don't stop reading and just hear me out -
I'm going to take you back to a time when I was much younger, 18-years-old to be exact.

I grew up a block away from Lake Superior and have had the convenience of being able to walk to the beach whenever I wanted throughout my entire life and what a great blessing it's been.

So, when I was 18, I had a particularly bad bout of depression but swimming at the beach just made sense and helped me clear my mind. The only strange thing is that I always liked to go at night when there was no one around so that I had time to just swim. I thought it was peaceful.

But I will never forget the night of October 26, 2003. It was a cold and windy and the moon was low in the sky. The waves were crashing and the water felt like ice. It just so happens that on that night my depression really took its toll on me.

TROY GRAHAM

I had to go swimming whether it killed me or not.
So there I went... I dove in head first, body surfing on all those magnificent waves and focusing on getting my feelings of inadequacy and misunderstanding out, until-before I knew it SHLOOOOOOP.

I was sucked right underwater by the distant and nonjudgemental undertow. I was flailing frantically and doing everything I could to get above water again but the harder I tried, the more pointless my struggle seemed.

So I accepted my fate and said to myself: "It's okay, let it take you, Troy, you can't win this fight."

Then all of a sudden, from beneath the water, something grabbed me from underneath my arms and just threw me out of the undertow.

I started to cough and spew up all of the water I ingested, but I was too tired from trying to swim out of the undertow that my arms and legs gave way.

I was just floating, waiting for the lake to suck me in again. It was right at that moment when I felt someone grab ahold of me and drag me onto shore.

I was so weak I could barely sit up, but when I finally got the strength all I could see were the faces of two devastatingly beautiful women, or so I thought. They just looked at me and smiled as I was catching my breath.

When I was finally able to speak again I said: "Were you two the ones who just dragged me out of the lake?"

They said "Yes."

I replied to them with tears of joy in my eyes, "Thank you, the two of you have saved my life!" I asked them for their names and where they had come from.

The one with red hair and a long beautiful smile told me her name was Yasmina and the other with long brown hair and eyes of no return said, "My name is Cecelia." They were sisters and Yasmina told me they had come from the lake.

I replied, "You mean the lake house?"

"No," they said, and then got as far out of the water as they could to show me their mermaid fins, "We are fresh water mermaids."

Then Yasmina said, "Me and my sister are the princesses of The Great Lakes and we have saved you because we needed to deliver you a message.

The message is: we know you have been struggling lately and have not had the best of luck, but we have just saved you from the undertow because it is not your time yet. The lake is not allowed to claim you, not on this night at least."

They told me I had a great, many things to do yet. That though my time on this Earth would not always be easy that I must stay around until it is my time to go. They said nothing more and disappeared into the water and I never saw them again.

I fell asleep on the beach that night from exhaustion and confusion, only to wake the next morning with the sun peaking over the rocks and I said to myself, "I'm still here so I better get busy living, it's the least I can do after what Yasmina and Cecelia did for me."

So here I am at age 36, still not sure where or how I will end up but

TROY GRAHAM

I know that I'm still alive and alive I will stay till it's my time to go.

Listen to the wind as it sings,
Listen to the rain as it falls for all of us out there
When it is our time, we will hear it call.

SUNRISE

As I watch the sunrise devour
What's left of the moon
I remember the last mistake I made
Was the day I thought I loved you
Rain dripping down from the drain pipes
Outside my house
I'll be the silent one in this story
I'll be quiet as a mouse

STARING

Staring at the empty road you left behind
Makes me realize that you are gone
I often think of the things we did
Drinking beer and singing songs
"Hold on to hope" is what you used to say to me
When I was down on my luck
You passed at 36 years old
And on that day, I heard angels sing
I believe you are somewhere better now
And that this world just
Was not good enough for you
I'm not sad anymore because I know you are the
Halo around the moon

SOBER OCTOBER

One more sober October
Seeing the leaves fall off the trees
And the feeling of the bitter wind
Coming in from the north

One more sober October
And I see all the people of the world
Dealing with their problems by using
Alcohol and drugs

One more sober October
Swimming with freshwater mermaids
In the largest body of freshwater
There has ever been

One more sober October
Being able to clearly see
What is right and what is wrong
Maybe next October I'll be sober
Or maybe I'll be gone

SISTER

I remember when I was a young boy
My sister would take and hide all my toys
She would not give them back until
I played the games she wanted to play
So she would use me as her dress-up doll
And make me play house all day
She would make me wear a dress and heels
Until I felt so strange that I would cry
Well guess what sis, jokes on you because now I know
Woman dig a guy who's in touch
With his feminine side
My sister was bigger than me so I had to play along
But I bet she didn't think I'd grow up
To write poems and songs
Sister you weren't nice to me then
But I forgive you now
I have not seen you in 8 years
So you could be just another face in the crowd
Maybe I'll see you again but then again maybe not
Good luck, sis, watch out for the clouds
They're all that remain in your heart's dim lit town

SILHOUETTES OF DREAMS

Through the doorway late at night
Is where the wind comes to chill my bones
It's late October and the ground is covered in snow
It's true when I was a child I felt
So misunderstood and alone
Things are better now
But it is still cold so leave me alone
Oh demons, because now you make me feel so old
Because of you, demons, I will spend the rest of my
Life trying to avoid the bumps in the road

SAILBOAT

Our love was like a sailboat
With no wind left in the sails
So do me a favor, keep your new
Love life to yourself
And save me the details

ROMANTIC

What is more romantic than the soft kiss
of the wind among the trees?
It's like I remember when you first looked at me
From your smile to your legs and your mysterious eyes
When you are around it's hard for me to focus my mind
What is more romantic than
A piece of chalk making love
To the sidewalk where it makes its art
How about when you reached
through my chest and touched my heart?
What is more romantic than when the reflection
in the clear lake is the moon?
The only thing that is the most romantic is simply you

RELIABLE

Love is tragic
Death is tragic, as well
The only difference to me
Between love and death is
Death is reliable and will come for us all
Love is a privilege not a right
So if you are lucky enough to be loved
Then be grateful every single day
And do your best to never let go

QUOTES

To follow your dreams
Is to be brave
So I hope
You are brave forever

To die is to live again
To be born is the day
You begin to die

PUBLIC TOILET

I'd rather clean a public toilet
Than give you the time of day
So do me a favor and stay the hell away
How many times must you do
That brilliant dance
And convince me to stay
How long before I just walk away
Nighttime is now here
With no light from the day
Nothing you say or do
Will make me lose my way
This is goodnight and -
It's all ok

PORCELAIN EYES

I see all the tears that you cry
When I look into your porcelain eyes
You were made in some factory
In Vermont a long time ago
You made a child happy once
But now you are just a doll
Sitting on a shelf
That has not been thought of in years
Maybe a garage sale will be your sweet escape
To another happy home
And another child who loves you
But until then I will see all the tears
You will cry from your porcelain eyes
Goodbye

POOL CLEANER

I once knew a man who used to clean
My outdoor public pool
His name was Jack and I liked hanging out
With Jack and drinking beer on the pool deck after
The pool had closed
I Hung out with Jack for about 2 years
jack would tell me his life story
How he was married once, how he had one kid
And how he was content with
His life as a pool cleaner
Then in late autumn 2006
When all the leaves had fallen and the pool was
Closed for another season
Jack passed away
Now from early-May to late-October I clean the
Pool that Jack once cleaned
I drink 2 beers on the pool deck every night
One for him and one for me
That seems to be the best way to remember the
Times I spent with old Jack
I'lI miss you, Jack, I'll keep the pool as clean as you did

PANDEMIC

Sunrise means nothing
In a world of darkness

August 1 2020

OUTHOUSE

A rainbow shining through the air vent
In the outhouse I'm sitting in
Makes the smell of shit
More tolerable than
If there was no rainbow at all

ORPHANS OF LOVE

Misunderstood, misguided, and oftentimes depressed
There are so many people who just feel like giving up
And wondering until they find
What they think they're looking for
The truth is, there are so many
Orphans of love out there
Who feel like love abandoned them so long ago
They feel as if they are the only ones who have
This deep dark place that no one else knows
And that the world or love
Could never understand them
So I say to you now - all ye orphans of love
If you let it in, love will find you again and again
Trust me I was an orphan of love once myself

NIGHT THOUGHTS

Fast moving, through time
Daylight disappears from the sky
It's only night
In this place I call home
Hope no longer exists
Silence and make-believe
What do they sound like
Your eyes show me oceans never swam
Your heart beats insecurities
Through lost memories
Now is your time I said to her
So live it and live it well

MY CAT

My cat is a loyal friend
My cat is always there
My cat is never a burden
My cat has the softest hair
My cat is the best example
Of not giving a f*ck
My cat is a good boy
But unlike many people
My cat does not suck

MOON GLOW

Far above the rainbow in the sky
The moon looks down and has no reply
We all came from stars so I have nothing to say
I feel sometimes as if I could be living in hell
The moon lingers above the rainbow in the sky
Waiting for its turn to sleep and for the sun to rise

MIND GAMES

Crows are tattooed on the statue of liberty
And the wine bottle cemetery is lying
Beneath the city lights
Reflecting off the water in late October
Where daytime lovers and nighttime drunks
Are all the same
Plastic smiles etched inside postline dreams
Where do I go from here?
The pain of enduring the judgement
Of so many people
Every single day
Is damn near intolerable

There is a fresh cut watermelon
On a skateboard in front of my house
Someone must have left that there last night
And I'm not sure what it means
There is a funeral taking place in my mind
For all the memories of my past
Let them die and please let their death last
The night turns to day
And the day turns to night
Where do I go from here
There is no destination in sight
So much darkness and a little bit of light

MARBLE MASK

Her marble mask is something
I could never quite see through
So I will swim in the sea
Until the tide brings me home to you
As I hear the cry of the starlings
Near a lighthouse
Where they have built their home
It's clear to me now that your eyes smile
And the years to come
Will never leave me alone

BLEACH

Bleach my heart
With your deceiving smile
Then undress my soul
With your soft touch

CHRISTMAS IN JULY

The clouds have created God's mustache
As the wind shouts like a car engine
In a swimming pool
It's Christmas in July again
There is bird shit all over
The dive bar in the middle of the street
Seems like a good place to hide from
All of the people consumed by the dandelion grove
I took a piss in the outhouse that was stuck inside
an elevator, I felt new after that
Then I attended the costume party
In the cemetery, where I found that
Doing ballet drunk is very hard
There is no time to climb the television tree
Holding the tire swing prisoner as the crows
Are laughing at the branches beneath their feet
It's Christmas in July again
Playing twister naked always turns into sex
Freshly cut grass I'm laying in reminds me
Of the time I dreamed of raincoats
Falling from the sky, the days when I still had hope

CAT

Cat chasing a ball of yarn never did me no harm
Cat is content sitting in the window watching cars
Cat never did me no harm
Cats like to eat, sleep, and play all day
Seems to me, cats are much like people
Just less in a way

CHANGE

Waiting for change every day
People tell me to be optimistic
But I've seen hate my whole life
People who stay in jobs and relationships
When they don't want to be
I've seen people fight in the middle of the street
One had a wrench, one had a baseball bat
When will things change?
The moon still glows
Reflects in the still pond at night
Daylight will always be the last thing in sight
But when will people love each other again?
I ask for things to change
But, at this point, I will take all the suffering
Coming to an end

CHALK DRAWING

You remind me of a chalk drawing in the rain
There is so much of you that has been washed away
From your face to your eyes
You have now completely left my brain
I thought all goodness was over
But now I see much brighter days
Ever since I found out you are nothing more
Then a chalk drawing in the rain

HATE

Hate is a waste of time
Hate can be over a nickel or dime
Hate is a dark passion and can
Influence people's hearts and minds
Hate is anger mixed with regret
Hate is the worst hate crime
That I've seen yet

GREEN CANDLE

Green candle in front of me is the only light I see
Because everything else is dark
Green candle in front of me is the only light I see
And it smells of evergreen and pine
Seems to me, like the light
Likes to waste the darkness's time
Green candle in front of me is the only light I see
So I guess I really am f*cked

GOD'S CANVAS

The sky is God's canvas where he paints
Pictures of mermaids dancing
In the sunrise of the morning
I can't remember which way is up
And which way is down
The cocaine and whisky flood the street
And the daytime darkness is all around
If you listen closely you will hear
Not a single pin drop
Where do we go from here?
I have not the answer for you
But if you want to live
Then you must do what -
You must do

GO AWAY

Go away and find where you think you'll be happy
Go away and pretend like no one loves you
Go away and you will see it's no better where you are
When you went away, you lived in your car
You came back home and now you sit
On a Tuesday night in a dimly lit bar

SILENCE

Do you hear the silence
Can you see the darkness
Can you feel the emptiness
That dwells inside you
If so you are a lot like me

YOUR BODY

Your body is my peaceful death
A land without mistakes and no regret
Your body is what I think of both day and night
Too bad I don't have your body to keep me warm
On these dark cold December nights

2ND HAND SLUMBER

Bath water draining while I sit in the tub
And have a heart that has no understanding of love
This is my 2nd hand slumber
Depression lasting from early November to late April
And a constant reminder that you're gone
This is my 2nd hand slumber
Christmas tree lights all faded and dim
And the vision of bad times to come
Summer - oh sweet summer, what have you done?
This is my 2nd hand slumber
Jake tells me she is dead and he wishes he was, too
Ham sandwich with no mayo
And bread that's past due
This is my 2nd hand slumber
So, tell me now, my friends,
Where do we all go from here?
Because this is just another dark,
Cold, Slow-moving year
This is my 2nd hand slumber

6 - WORD POEMS

Crowded streets
Hate everywhere
Darkness falling

Overwhelmed yet untouched
Uncontrollable tears lost

Ashtray full
Alcohol gone
Time wasted

Fall faster
Beneath the trees
Daydreaming

Take my hand
Take my heart

6 - WORD POEMS (CONT.)

Love long, Love true, Love always

The time moves fast through life

My mind has lost its way

The wind blows hard in October

Bleeding trees
Bleeding hearts
Bloody streets

BEDROOM OF BROKEN DREAMS

In my bedroom of broken dreams
Is where I first realized I was a drunk and wasted
7 years of my life
In my bedroom of broken dreams
Is where I used to dance with the idea of suicide
In my bedroom of broken dreams
Is where I had to swallow my pride

In my bedroom of broken dreams
It is just me, myself, and I
In my bedroom of broken dreams
Is where I learned to cry

In my bedroom of broken dreams
Is where I would ask myself why -
Why is it easier for me to just run and hide?

ALL

Trees growing
Years passing
Friends dying
Night clashing with day
All things being what they are
This is life, the circle
Of all things
Or so we think

BELLS

The bells that ring at the start of a wedding
Are the same as the bells that ring
At the start of a funeral
So here I sit at your wedding
And all I can think about is death

BOBBY FISCHER

You were an unparalleled genius in the game of chess
Who never really loved anyone, more or no less
Chess was anger, pain, frustration, beauty, and
All that ever made sense to you
For years, you disappeared because
You couldn't handle the weight of the world
But you came back to show that you
Were still the best and then vanished again
You are gone now, but will never be forgotten as
The grand master you were

BLUE JAY

Watching the street lights burning
As I walk home at 6 a.m.
Here I am, hungover again
Leaving some strange woman's house
I am barefoot and look across the street
When I see a blue jay
On the step of my neighbor's porch
The bird is trying to get in
A carved pumpkin by removing the
Top with its beak
So that it can stay warm
But the bird is unsuccessful
It's October and I'm freezing
Standing outside in this godforsaken cold
I guess now I know how the bird must feel
At least for a moment

DISTANCE

All I see is distance these days
Distance between what you ask?
Distance between her heart and his smile
Distance between people and the words they say
And most importantly distance between
Action and comprehension
So little love and so much pain
There are not enough umbrellas
For all the world's rain
Or maybe it's just not enough
Blood circulating through the brain
Or maybe it's just a brand new sweater with a
Brand new stain
Tomorrow things may be distant
But at least it's a new day

DEATH

Death is not fair, death is everywhere
Death will be the one to pick when it is your time
Death does not care whether it is day or night
Death will carry you away through the wind
When you experience death a new life can begin
Death is the perfect example of pain
Death is in each little drop of rain
Death is a certain chill and always there
So is that death
Or just the wind blowing through your hair?

DAYDREAMS AND DENTAL FLOSS

My life is seen through the eyes
Of a third-century cat while
It's taking an afternoon nap
I have the most fun when I play hopscotch
Next to the lemonade stand in the creek bed
Daydreams and dental floss is where I belong
The wheelbarrow in my yard is filled with
Ice and beer and the sun is setting on the
Skin of a barebacked woman
Daydreams and dental floss is where I belong
The lounge chair looks like toilet paper
Stretched around the moon as the water
Tastes like cement and the bus driver
Eats a hotdog sandwich
While I look for cigarette butts
To smoke on a 95-degree day
I'm sweating whisky and thinking of her body
I look like a polar bear in the desert
Dental floss and daydreams is where I belong

DARK MORNING

Slipping with every step I take
Walking down the hill on a cold January morning
I can see my breath
My fingers are numb
It's so dark I rely on the street lights to lead the way
My feet press down on fresh patches of snow
It's 6 a.m. and I'm not sure where I should go
There's very little sound and
The dawn is breaking now
I'm dancing with depression
To the songs of a snow plow
I am alone and the wind whispers
"Welcome to the club"
When I get home,
　I'll hear the silence of not being loved

CROSSING THE RIVER

Crossing the river where many people have drowned
Crossing the river where the weeds at the bottom
Try to grab hold of my legs and drag me down
Crossing the river where I feel the muck
And sand beneath my toes
Crossing the river, I'm not sure if I'll ever make it home
Rain, sleet, hail, and snow
What's across the river?
At this rate, it seems like I'll never know

COLD PROS

Let the wind blow where it may

All those who do evil
Will have their judgment day

I've seen so much bad and so little good
That now I have nothing to say

I do my best to overcome the madness
And find a better way

I will always love you, my dear
And in my heart you will stay

COFFIN DUST

It's all black stairs and coffin dust
When I see you at 3 a.m.
So many tulips falling from the sky
Summer is setting the plot for
The disaster in your eyes
All of these long, cold, wet summer days
My only explanation is the devil is doing ballet

GLASS HOUSE

The man who is made of stone is living in a glass house

How much longer will this madness last?

Trees dying
People dying
and the masses are
Lost and there is so much evil

In seclusion, but not by choice
Late at night, when I listen closely,
I can hear the voice
The voice of who or what I'll never know

So step right up, one and all, and
Get your ticket to the horror show

FORGOTTEN DREAMS

High over the sleeping mountains
Is where dreams go when they are forgotten
The lonely man tends to his garden
And hears the sound of no one else around
I have dreams, I have love to give
And would like a partner to bathe in a fountain with
I have my best thoughts when I'm high over the
Sleeping mountains
He could kiss your lips or dry your eyes
Or hold your hand whenever you cry
He could be there day and night
And whenever you feel sad
He could take you high over the sleeping mountains
Whenever you feel bad
He thought his dreams were forgotten
But now all of them are with you
High over the sleeping mountains
Is where you will find the truth

FLOOD

Let your eyes see
The flood of tears
I cry for your love

FINDING

Cold night in November
Where I was going, I can't remember
Tears from the wind as I walk outside
Tears when I get home because
I have nowhere to hide
Hide from what, you ask?
Sometimes the world
Sometimes the snow
Will hiding do any good, you ask?
I just don't know

FACE DOWN

As she lies face down in a swimming pool
In her best friend's backyard
She is thinking I can't do it anymore
And I'm done trying
Let the water enter my lungs
And take me somewhere more peaceful
Than this selfish, hateful world
4 days later we buried her in the ground
We all wept
What was it for
Whatever was it for?

HATE PT. 2

Hate is simple so I dare you to love
To not care is easy, so I dare you to care
Tonight the wind is strong
As it's blowing through the air
Putting the blame on someone else is easy and
The sun is setting fast
So I say take responsibility
For what you have done
And don't dwell on the past

LIFE IN MIND

Some nights are mornings
And some mornings are just a continuation of the night
It's hard to always keep my head up
And find what is right
The poet is growing older and
the painter is getting tired
With all that is happening in this world
I have no problem being inspired
My wounds were deep and my scars still remain
No matter how unclear things seem
I can still feel the rain

LOST AND LOST

Her mood was the same as that of a beached whale
Being her friend is the same as walking home alone
The feeling of nothingness and the hard truth
Of what your life has become
As she is all alone now
And thinks - "What have I done?"

LIFE

Live forever in the wind that blows
Live for always in the trees that stand
There is endless life in each grain of sand
Love death, forever - it's all in God's hands

LAKE SUPERIOR

Great Lake Superior is a cemetery
Of souls that have been
Killed in its undertow
For so many years

Great Lake Superior can be like
Looking at yourself in a mirror
And then its murderous waves could be
Crashing against the breakwall the same night

The sound of Great Lake Superior in the wind
Is what makes me hold my pillow tight

Great Lake Superior can be kind by day
And then unforgiving by night

Great Lake Superior has shown
Me the coldest moon I've ever seen
Time after time after time

LADDER

Climb the ladder to find what you are looking for
Climb the ladder to see the stars
Climb the ladder to reach a book
Climb the ladder for a good look
Lay the ladder down over wet cement
So you don't have to
Leave any footprints behind
Climb the ladder so you can see what's on my mind
I would climb the ladder, too
But I simply haven't got the time

IMMORTAL REALITY

Suicide is death's playmate
Like the wind is the earth's
It's hard to see anything anymore
In this God forsaken town
One 24-hour laundromat
One bar that's open till 2 a.m.
It's difficult to know where bad
Dreams end and hell begins
I'm a slave to money and to your deceiving eyes
I just wish I could awake from this nightmare I call life
I'm always in darkness, making it hard to see the light
Many times I've been hurt so it's also hard to be kind
I've been told that to love is wasteful so oh,
How I love to waste my time
Maybe I'm just growing older or
Maybe I've just lost my mind

I'VE LOST MY MIND AGAIN

Sledge hammer hitting the ground
Cargo box filled with pears and grapes
wet flore signs in the grocery store aisles
Gum stuck to the bottom of my shoe
Men sniffing flowers in the field across the way
Clouds pissing down rain
Holy shit, it's been one hell of a day
Thump thump thud crash roar
It's thunder and lightning
It's a big damn storm
Man running out of the store
Stealing beer, committing a crime
I'm glad I just woke up
Because I sure can't handle my mind

I'M LOST

In a room full of God
I see dracula standing in the corner
Wanting my blood
The wind chimes outside are jangling
My mind is a dark place of no return
I hear all of the voices laughing
Laughing, laughing...
Please help me make it stop
In this room full of God
I can't see anything except
Dracula still standing in the corner
And the silhouettes of flies ready to hover
I have chills because even though it's hot outside
It's cold beneath these covers
I'm cold, I must go to sleep
Good night, sweet sorrow
Good night

THE STEEPLE

Through the cathedral steeple
Sun shines down onto the
Sidewalk where I stand
If we have the need to feel wanted again
We can just hold on to each other's hands
To fill the void of so many lovers
And good times lost
Through the cathedral steeple
Sun shines down on to
What is real and what is not

YOUR LOVE

Oh, how your love surrounds me
Like a sea filled with acrobatic sharks
That have just tasted blood for the first time
I've never been more scared in my life
The soft glow of the television
Reflecting off the living room floor
Reminds me of a starlings nest filled
With dental floss and old dirt
What more can I say
Another breath
Another thought
Here comes the rain

This is my average day

YOUR EYES

Your eyes give me hope when I feel all is lost
Your eyes are like a ship on the ocean
That sees no sign of shore
Your eyes are like an endless field of flowers
Looking in your eyes
Gives me the answer to questions
That most of the time take hours
Your eyes are one of the only things
 I know to be bright and true
Your eyes - oh, those eyes, are what made
Me fall in love with you

WHY?

Why is there war
Why is the sky blue
Why have so many of my friends died
Please God tell me it's not true
Why is there so much hate and so little love
Why are there so many angry people
 Shedding so much blood
Why are oak trees tall and
Why is the the grass green
Looks like asking why is a waste of time
At least from what I've seen

WHERE IS THE LOVE?

Where is the love?
Love does not exist on the streets where I dwell
Some people say this is heaven on earth but
I believe we are living in hell
You can find me alone in my house
Bidding you farewell
People have run out of love
And I just can't take it anymore
Once I stood up straight
Now I lay on the floor
Sun, shine on me again and show me brighter days
I oftentimes feel like the people of the world
Where I have lost my way
But at least I get to try another day

TRUTHS

Her smile alone could bring angels to their knees
But when she smiles at 3 a.m. she smiles just for me
From her shiny long hair
To the reflection of my face in her eyes
I was the first to tell her she was beautiful
And that it's okay to be shy
Now I've gone to be with my lover and
I'll need to close the blinds
As my shadow shrinks from the ground
In the late afternoon
I'll say farewell and goodnight

TODAY

Today I was walking down the street
When I saw her eyes
Her eyes remind me of a piece of gum
On the bottom of someone's shoe
That a family of ants is about to make there harvest
So needless to say I do not like her eyes
Or her tree vomit ballyhoo

WINDMILL

Don't ask me why I'm sitting here by this river bed
How could anyone really understand
What I've been through
I'm like a windmill meant to stand
Alone on any occasion
Hot sun, freezing cold winter, bad rain storm
Always left alone to do the jobs
No one else wants to do
And lots of jobs no one will ever see the value in
I'm here to be this misunderstood
Creature of the night
That will always do the final job
Whatever that may be
I'm like a windmill and I'll never be free

TIME

I am the ruler and
eventual death, extinction of all living things
I control where you go and what you do
I am the reason for the darkest of nights
And for the sun that rises in the day
I am a prison sentence
Or the life of a car
The tide coming in on the beach
And I beat high mountains down
I am time

THE TREMBLING WIND

The trembling wind beneath my feet
Makes the ground I'm standing on feel weak
The moon glow makes me alive inside
I am destined for darkness but still have found love
My eyes grow tired, my knees grow weak
It's so cold outside, I can barely speak
Too much time has past for me
To forget what you have done
I feel as if most of the world is breathing
Through dishonest lungs
The chill in my bones and the pain in my back
The trembling wind beneath my feet
When did we all get so far off track?

THE TREES

The trees look like the smiles of all my dead friends
The leaves are wet and stuck to the ground
The days are long and dark and have no sign of hope
The fork in the sugar bowl is good for nothing
The dinosaurs are still alive in my mind
The ventriloquist is moving his lips
When the dummy speaks
Come home if you want or stay gone if it feels right
The silhouettes are silent and move during the night
The trees look like the faces of all my dead friends
So tell me when will the hate, regret, and madness
Come to an end?

TWO ROSES

Two roses red as blood I left at your door
Two letters never read
I wish I could have done more
Your smile is like the sun in my eyes
Or the burning in my heart
Dying feelings, what a beautiful work of art
Hollow homes
All alone and the rooms the moonlight shines on
I think and hope
That someday you'll be sorry when I'm gone

WHAT THE HELL

There is cake on the floor and beer in the sink
I'm so hungover yet I could really use a drink
I'm high as a kite and as low as the bottom of the sea
I'm losing my mind and you are losing me
Darkness and darkness more and more
Every time I have a nightmare
It begins with cake on the floor

TIME FREQUENCY

The years have passed by
Like water through a screen
But no matter how dark it gets,
I still have my dreams
Dreams of music, poetry, and dreams of you
Dreams of what's to come, and what's true
At the end of each day, no matter what is wrong,
I still have you
I drank for years, smoked, and had no hope in sight
I even remember when I thought
I didn't know wrong from right
I lived for awhile in the day
But mostly now it is the night
Dreaming seemed wrong for a while
But now it seems right
I got you and you got me dear
So hold on tight

TOWER

You are like the tower I will never be able to reach
Turns out that you are like the tower
That makes my knees so weak
You're the loss of appetite in a late night diner
Or the sparkle that has faded from my eyes
So pardon me, but you are the reason I always cry

I LOVE YOU

I love you in the way that the shadow loves the light
I love you the same as the darkness loves the night
I need you the way the wind needs a kite
I love you more each day I know this is right
I need you like a flower needs the ground
There is so much love in our hearts
I feel it all around
Day has come and night will pass
The one thing I truly believe is that
Our love surely will last

For my wife

HOPSCOTCH

Hopscotch is the game we would play
In the cemetery when we were drunk
Hopscotch is the game we would play
To forget all the shit of this world
The rich get richer and the poor get poorer
We play hopscotch now
Because that seems to all make total sense

HOPE

I'm sure it seems like to have hope
Is hopeless during this time of death and sorrow
But remember if you have hope today
You may just see tomorrow
Pray often and pray on your knees
I truly believe if we have hope and faith
We will beat this disease

LOST LOST LOST

Your eyes are the vacant parking lot
Of an abandoned store
Your words cut like a knife and
 I can hear them no more

Your smile is lost somewhere between
Happiness and regret
You think there is no hope but
I know things will get better yet

Empty heart, empty bed,
And so many tears I've seen you cry
Your loneliness was beyond repair
So I had to say goodbye

LOST

When I see you now after 3 years of
Being in a relationship
You look about as hot as 20-minute-old bath water
And you have the same expression on your face as a
Piece of melted liquorice
On a 90-degree day
The piece of bread on the sidewalk is
Being eaten by ants
What the hell have you
Been through these last 3 years?
Oh wait, I don't care

TAKE THE TIME

Take the time to hear the screams
Take the time to see the pain
Take the time to fall in love
Take the time to feel the rain
River running fast
River running wide
Take the time to really see
The world for what it is
And I bet you will run and hide

STEAM GHOST

I can see the steam ghosts
Running on the cold streets in late March
There is a cat on the chair in my living room
Just pur pur purring away
 And the yellow blob of my reality bleeds purple blood
After all that being said
Steam ghosts don't seem that bad
Goodnight wanderers
For answers, look to the sky

THE RAIN

The people are lying, the people are crying
What's the problem with this world?
The wind blows hard, the night is cold
The earth shakes, the streets are empty
The sun rises but still I see nothing changing
The rich getting richer - the poor getting poorer
When will things change - soon, I hope?
The only thing I can rely on
To always be the same
Is the rain
The rain when it floods the streets,
The rain when it pours down
The rain when it makes you
Feel a little less alone in your town
The rain when you shiver, the rain when it's cold
I may be young now, but unlike the rain
All the hate I see is getting old

THE FIFTH FLOOR

It's so loud - the sound of the washing machines
Pounding on the ground
The laundry room is a hollow, dim place
Soda bottles people have left behind
On the 5th floor of your apartment building
Is where my senses go blind
I have a book and the smell of detergent
To get me through
Washing my clothes is a whole lot better
Than having to spend my time with you
I found a bandana and someone's lonely left shoe
All I know for sure is
My time spent on the 5th floor
Is haunting yet true

THE DICE YOU ROLL

I am nothing more than the dice you roll
And that's all I can promise you
You will be taking a chance on me
And I'll be taking a chance on you
I will love you until I die and always do my best
So don't worry about the dice you roll and give
Your heart a rest

THE TIRE SWING

It's been ten years since I've seen that tire swing
Hanging from the tree
Behind the church next to my house
I fell to my knees in tears
Thinking of the last time I saw
That old tire swing -
It just so happens to be the same day
My friend Julia hung herself on the tree branch next
To where the swing was,
Which is why I fell to my knees in tears
Now that I see it again

ABOUT THE AUTHOR

Troy Graham

Troy is a poet, singer-songwriter from Marquette, MI. This is his fourth published poetry book since 2015. Troy enjoys traveling to libraries near and far, teaching interactive poetry workshops and performing all ages folk concerts.

For more information visit him at:
facebook.com/troygrahammusic

Made in the USA
Columbia, SC
15 January 2022